Common Core
Classification

By Carole Marsh
Published by Gallopade International, Inc.
©Carole Marsh/Gallopade
Printed in the U.S.A. (Peachtree City, Georgia)

TABLE OF CONTENTS

G: Includes Graphic Organizer

GO: Graphic Organizer is also available 8½" x 11" online
         download at www.gallopade.com/client/go
(numbers above correspond to the graphic organizer numbers online)

What Is Classification?

Read the text and answer the questions.

To "classify" means to divide into groups. You might classify your clothes into two groups—summer clothes and winter clothes… or dirty clothes and clean clothes. You also could classify cars in a parking lot—perhaps by color, year, or model. The process of dividing things into groups is called <u>classification</u>.

People classify things into different groups by studying how they are similar and how they are different. Summer and winter clothes share many similarities, but winter clothes keep you warm, and summer clothes keep you cool. Scientists use a similar method of comparison to classify all living organisms into different groups.

Scientists classify organisms into groups to show how organisms are related to each other. For example, think of all life on Earth as belonging to one big family. Some organisms are closely related (like a brother or sister) and others very distantly related (like a distant cousin). Scientists study their characteristics to determine how to classify them into groups. Organisms that are classified in the same group are closely related to each other.

Scientists study the fossilized remains of organisms that lived in the past, too, to explain the family tree of all life on Earth. One organism that lived in the past could be closely related to several different organisms that are alive today!

1. A. Use the text to define <u>classification</u>.
   B. Describe the process of classification.
   C. Why do scientists classify living organisms?

2. A. What analogy is used to describe the relationship between all organisms on Earth?
   B. In your opinion, why was this analogy used?

3. A. Which items below could be classified as "sports equipment"?
   B. Which items below could be classified as "spheres"?

APPLYING CONCEPTS

Can You Classify?

Look at the list and answer the questions.

THIS WEEK'S GROCERY LIST

1 pound of ground beef	4 tomatoes
6 pears	1 package of chicken wings
2 packages of bacon	1 large watermelon
1 gallon of milk	6 red apples
1 head of lettuce	1 small pineapple
4 squash	12 ounces of cream cheese
2 pound of salmon	2 pound of tuna fish
1 head of broccoli	1 bunch of spinach

1. Complete the graphic organizer by classifying the items on the grocery list. First, classify them into two broad groups. Then classify them into the smaller, more specific groups.

All Food on Grocery List

Food from plants:

Food from animals:

Fruit (part of plant with seeds):

Vegetables (part of plant without seeds):

Meat (made from animal muscle):

Dairy (made from animal milk):

2. Which level uses more characteristics to classify the items?

3. Think of another way to divide the grocery list into your own system of classification. Choose your categories based on similarities and differences. You can be creative! Draw a diagram of your system of classification, classify all of the items on the grocery list, and share your results with your class.

©Carole Marsh/Gallopade • www.gallopade.com • page 3

How to Classify

Read the text and answer the questions.

Scientists classify organisms by comparing and contrasting their <u>traits</u>. Traits are used to group organisms together or to tell two organisms apart. Some traits, like physical traits, are easy to see. Genetic traits require advanced scientific tools to study.

Early scientists used their eyes as well as simple tools to compare and classify organisms by their similarities. They studied outward physical traits like size, color, and weight, as well as inward physical traits such as skeletal structure, how the organisms digests food, and how it changes throughout its life cycle.

Studying physical traits is still an important part of classification today, but it is only the first step. If two organisms share similar physical traits, scientists investigate further to discover whether or not the two organisms have a common ancestor. This is an important step because two organisms may look very similar, but they may not be related at all.

In the early 20th century, scientists discovered that parents pass traits to their offspring through structures called genes. Scientists later discovered that genes are made of DNA that control an organism's genetic traits. Today, scientists use laboratory equipment to study and categorize an organism's complete DNA. Organisms that share similar DNA often look similar, too, but DNA evidence is a more accurate way to tell if two organisms are related. DNA from living organisms can be compared to fossilized DNA of extinct organisms to identify common ancestors as well.

1. A. Use the text to define <u>traits</u>.
    B. Why do scientists look for similarities in organisms' traits?
    C. Why do scientists look for differences in organisms' traits?

2. List at least five ways that scientist compare and contrast traits.

3. How does fossilized evidence help scientists classify organisms?

4. Cite evidence from the text to support the inference: "Looks can be deceiving."

5. Imagine you have discovered a new organism. In a well-organized paragraph, explain what steps you would take to classify it.

Classifying by Observation

Look at the photographs and answer the questions.

All photos courtesy of Wikimedia Commons

1. List at least five physical traits that all four animals have in common.

2. Complete the table by describing each animal's unique physical traits.

Organism	Unique Physical Traits
A Black Bear	
B Red Fox	
C Fennec Fox	
D Polar Bear	

3. Which pairs of organisms are most likely closely related? Why?

4. Classify these organisms into two groups and give each group a name. Cite similarities and differences to support your answers.

Comparing Two Systems

Read the documents and answer the questions

James Rennie wrote many books about the classification systems of organisms. In 1831, he wrote about the classification systems used by scientists who studied insects. These excerpts summarize the classification systems of scientists Clairville and Latreille.

Clairville's Classification of Insects

I. Winged Insects (Pterophora)
1. With jaws (mandibulata)
   a) With wing-cases
   b) With coriaceous wings
   c) With netted wings
   d) With veined wings

2. With suckers (Haustellata)
   a) Wings with poisers (Halteriptera)
   b) Wings powdery

II. Wingless Insects (Aptera)
1. With sucker (Haustellata)
   With a sharp sucker (Rophoptera)
2. With jaws (Mandibulata)
   With legs formed for running (Pododunera)

1. A. What is the first trait **Clairville** uses to classify insects?
   B. How many groups does this divide into? Why?

2. A. What trait does **Clairville** use to classify the insects in Group I?
   B. What trait does **Clairville** use to classify the insects in Group II?

3. A. What is the first trait **Latreille** uses to classify insects?
   B. How many groups does classification by this trait result in? Why?

4. A. What trait does **Latreille** use to classify the insects in Group I?
   B. What trait does **Latreille** use to classify the insects in Group II?

5. A. Draw a simple diagram showing **Clairville's** classification system.
   B. Draw a simple diagram showing **Latreille's** classification system.

Latreille's Classification of Insects

I. Insects with more than six feet, and without wings (Myriapoda)

    1. With many jaws—wood lice (Chilognatha)
    2. With many feet—millepedes (Chilopoda)

II. Insects with Six Feet (Aptera)

    1. Without wings :—
      a) With organs of motion like feet (Thysanura)
      b) Mouth with a retractile sucker (Parasita)
      c) External mouth with a jointed tube enclosing a sucker (suctoria)

    2. With four wings :—
    A. Upper wings crustaceous, at least at base
      a) With the under wings folded crosswise—beetles (Coleoptera)
      b) With the under wings folded lengthwise (Orthoptera)
        Legs formed for running (Cursoria)
        Legs formed for leaping (Saltatoria)
      c) With a sucker enclosing several bristles (Hemiptera)
    B. Upper wings membraneceous
      a) Wings naked and netted (Neuroptera)
      b) Wings naked and veined (Hymenoptera)
      c) Wings with dust-like scales (Lepidoptera)

    3. With two twisted elytra and two wings (Rhipiptera)
    4. With two wings (Diptera)

---

6. As additional traits are used to classify the insects:
   A. Are the insects in the new groups more similar or more varied than in the previous group?
   B. Are they more closely related or more distantly related than in the previous group?
   C. Are the groups becoming larger or smaller?

7. A. How are Clairville and Latreille's systems of classification similar?
   B. How are their systems of classification different?

8. In your opinion, which scientist's system of classification is more detailed and thorough? Explain why.

Why Classify?

Follow the instructions for Parts A and B.

PART A: Read the text and answer the questions.

The branch of science responsible for classifying and naming organisms is called <u>taxonomy</u>. The name taxonomy comes from the Greek word *"taxis"* which means "arrangement." <u>Taxonomists</u> arrange, or classify, similar organisms into a group, called a taxon.

There are many different <u>taxa</u> *(plural form of taxon)*. A taxon can be <u>broad</u> like the taxon *Animalia* that includes all animals. Or a taxon can be more <u>specific</u> like the taxon *Carnivora* that only includes animals that are meat-eating mammals.

Scientists group organisms that are biologically related into the same taxon. That way, scientists can easily recognize which organisms are most closely related to each other. Taxonomists also study the fossils of extinct organisms to determine how living organisms of the past are related to living organisms on Earth today, and group them into taxa, too.

1. Match each description with the word from the text it defines:
   A. The person who studies relationships between organisms.
   B. The biologically-related groups organisms can be arranged in.
   C. The science and method of classifying and naming organisms.

2. A. Identify which paragraph of the text best answers the question: "What is the purpose of taxonomy?"
   B. Use the text to answer the question.

3. Which word best describes the relationship between the words <u>broad</u> and <u>specific</u>? Explain.
   a) synonyms   b) homonyms   c) antonyms   d) metaphors

4. Number the following taxa from broadest (1) to most specific (4).
   A. _____ including only animals that have spines and are fish
   B. _____ including only animals that have spines
   C. _____ including all animals
   D. _____ only animals that have spines and are fish with jaws.

Every organism can be classified into seven taxonomic levels—kingdom, phylum, class, order, family, genus, and species. Each level identifies a taxon that the organism belongs to. The top level is a very broad taxon that includes many different organisms. Each level below is more and more specific, until the lowest level only includes one type of organism. This taxonomic system arranges organisms by placing them next to the organisms that are most closely related.

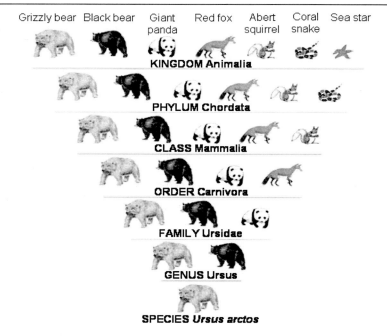

5. A. Describe the organization of this diagram.
   B. What is the purpose of having seven different levels?

6. A. Which level includes the broadest taxon? Name it.
   B. Which level includes the most specific taxon? Name it.

7. A. Which two organisms are animals, but not mammals?
   B. Why is the squirrel not included in the order *Carnivora*?

8. A. According to the diagram, which organism is **most** closely related to the grizzly bear?
   B. According to the diagram, which organism is the **least** closely related to the grizzly bear?

Kingdoms & Domains

Read the texts and answer the questions.

The system of classification and taxonomy that we use today began with Carl Linnaeus in the 1700s. Linnaeus divided all living organisms into two very broad groups called kingdoms—*Plantae* and *Animalia*. Scientists today still classify organisms as plants and animals, but many living organisms are not plants or animals. Since Linnaeus' time, scientists have discovered more about life on Earth and added more kingdoms. Today, most scientists use a system of classification with six kingdoms. However, the number of kingdoms could change if new species are discovered that do not fit in any of the current six kingdoms.

Plantae are multicellular organisms like trees and flowers. They have cells with a nucleus. Plant cells also have thick cell walls for support and chloroplasts that help make food from sunlight.

Animalia are multicellular organisms that can move. Like plant cells, animal cells contain a nucleus. However, animal cells do not have a cell wall or chloroplasts. Animals gain energy by eating food from plants or other animals. Animals range from small insects to the largest whale.

Fungi are similar to plants but have remarkable differences. Like plants, fungi are multicellular, except for yeasts, and have cells that contain a nucleus. Their cells have a cell wall like plants, but they do not contain chloroplasts or make food from sunlight. Instead, fungi are natural decomposers and gain energy from absorbing the nutrients of dead organisms.

Protista are microscopic unicellular organisms that have a nucleus. Protists come in a wide variety of forms. Some protists, like amoeba, are animal-like and can move. Some protists, like algae, are plant-like and cannot move and contain chloroplasts for photosynthesis.

Bacteria and **Archaea** are the simplest organisms, having only one cell and no nucleus. Bacteria and Archaea are very similar microscopic organisms. However, Archaea have different chemicals in their cells and tend to live in extreme environments. In fact, scientists believe archaea are closely related to the first life forms ever to exist on Earth.

1. What are the six kingdoms?

2. A. The prefix "multi" means "many." What can you infer about organisms that are <u>multicellular</u>?
    B. The prefix "uni" means "one." What can you infer about organisms that are <u>unicellular</u>?

3. Give at least two examples of how scientists use each of the following to classify organisms into kingdoms:
    A. number of cells   B. how it gains energy   C. cell structure

4. A. Compare and contrast plants and animals.
    B. What do plants, animals, fungi, and protists have in common?

5. Explain why a system of classification can change over time.

PART B: Read this text and answer the questions below.

> Many scientists recognize a taxonomic level above kingdom, called a domain. In fact, domains are the broadest taxonomic level and are sometimes called superkingdoms.
>
> Scientist group organisms from the six kingdoms into three large domains—Eurkarya, Bacteria, and Archaea—based on their cell structures. Eukarya contains organisms that are <u>eukaryotic</u>, which means they have cells with a nucleus. Bacteria and Archaea contain organisms that are <u>prokaryotic</u>, which means they have a cell without a nucleus.

6. A. Use the second text to define <u>eukaryotic</u>.
    B. Which kingdoms contain organisms that are eukaryotic?

7. A. Use the second test to define <u>prokaryotic</u>.
    B. Which kingdoms contain organisms that are prokaryotic?

8. Use information from both texts to complete the table.

Domain ➡	Archaea	Bacteria	Eukarya			
Kingdom			Protista			
Cell Type		No Nucleus			Nucleus	
Cell Number		Unicellular				
How organism gets energy	Varies	Varies	Varies			

Classification Report

Individually or in small groups, choose an organism to research that is also one of your state's symbols. Use online or classroom resources to identify the organism and its taxonomic classification. Explain what each level means and how the organism fits that classification on the lines provided.

Domain

_____

_____

_____

Kingdom

_____

_____

_____

Phylum (Division)

_____

_____

_____

Class

_____

_____

_____

State Bird   State Insect   State Reptile   State Fish

State Flower   State Wildflower   State Tree

Order

_____

_____

_____

Family

_____

_____

_____

Genus

_____

_____

_____

Species

_____

_____

_____

COMPARE & CONTRAST
Classifying Animals

Read the text and answer the questions.

The animal kingdom, or kingdom *Animalia*, is a very diverse group of organisms. Some animals live in the air, some on land, and some in the water. Different animals may have different physical characteristics, different life cycles, and different reproduction methods. Animals range from the smallest worms to the largest whales.

Although organisms in the kingdom *Animalia* vary greatly, all animals have key similarities. All animals are made of many eukaryotic cells. All animals have the ability to move their own bodies. All animals are consumers, meaning they must eat other organisms as food for energy.

Organisms in the kingdom Animalia can be classified into smaller groups. One of the first characteristics scientists use to classify animals into smaller groups is body structure. An important body-structure trait they look at is whether or not the animal has a backbone. Animals with a backbone are called vertebrates. Animals without a backbone are called invertebrates.

All vertebrates are in the phylum *Chordata*. Vertebrates typically have a strong skeletal system that is supported by the backbone. All mammals (animals that have fur or hair), including humans, are vertebrates. Birds, reptiles, amphibians, and fish also have backbones. Believe it or not, only about 10% of all animals in the animal kingdom have a backbone.

In contrast, about 90% of all animals are invertebrates. There are eight different phyla of invertebrates. Arthropods, mollusks, worms, and echinoderms are some of the different types of invertebrates. The phylum *Arthropoda* includes all invertebrates with jointed exoskeletons and at least three pairs of jointed legs. Insects, spiders, and crustaceans are in this category. The phylum *Mollusca* includes animals that usually have soft unsegmented bodies and shells. Snails and clams are examples of this category. The phylum *Annelida* includes long, slender invertebrates that have soft bodies and no limbs, such as worms. Other phyla classifications are based on traits such as pores, a single opening to the digestive system, and more!

PART A: For each question, identify which paragraph(s) includes information needed in order to answer it, and then answer the question.

1. _____ What traits do all animals have in common?
2. _____ What is a vertebrate?
3. _____ Are most animals vertebrates or invertebrates?
4. _____ How many phyla is the animal kingdom divided into?
5. _____ Are fish more closely related to mollusks or mammals?

PART B: Use the text to determine whether each statement is **true (T)** or **false (F)**. Rewrite each false statement to be true.

6. _____ The animal kingdom can be divided into smaller categories.
7. _____ The kingdom *Animalia* is a very narrow, specific taxon.
8. _____ The animal kingdom includes single and multicellular organisms.
9. _____ Vertebrate animals only live on land.
10. _____ Invertebrates do not have skeletons.

Complete the graphic organizer by comparing and contrasting vertebrates and invertebrates.

Vertebrates   **Invertebrates**

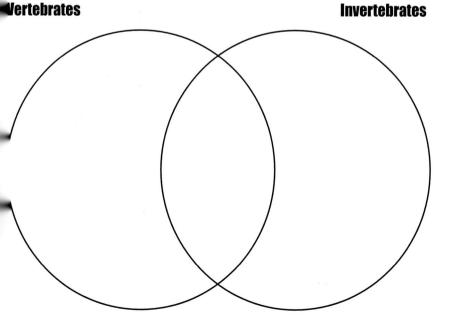

Vertebrates

Read the table and answer the questions.

Characteristics of Vertebrates (Animals with a Backbone)

Mammals	Reptiles	Amphibians
• has fur/hair • takes care of its young; mothers nurse the young • gives birth to its young • warm-blooded • has lungs	• has scales and not fur • rarely takes cares of its young • usually lays eggs • cold-blooded • has lungs	• has moist skin • has webbed feet • lays eggs • lives on land and in water • cold-blooded • has lungs

Birds	Fish
• has feathers and wings • takes care of its young for awhile • lays eggs • warm-blooded • has lungs	• has scales and fins • lives in water • breathes using gills • lays eggs • cold-blooded

1. List at least five physical characteristics used to classify vertebrates.

2. Which characteristics listed describe part of an animal's life cycle?

3. A. Classify the animals based on body temperature.
   B. Classify the animals based on how they breathe.

4. Which characteristics of mammals are unique to only mammals?

5. A. Explain how a fish's traits make it suited to a water habitat.
   B. Explain how a bird's traits make it suited to air and land habitats.

6. Use the table as well as an online resource to classify each of the following animals as either mammal, reptile, amphibian, bird, or fish.
   A. _____ cheetah
   B. _____ crocodile
   C. _____ porpoise
   D. _____ tree frog
   E. _____ cobra snake
   F. _____ bald eagle
   G. _____ tilapia
   H. _____ elephant
   I. _____ blue jay
   J. _____ seahorse
   K. _____ salamander
   L. _____ common toad

READING INFORMATIONAL TEXT

What Is a Species?

Read the text and answer the questions.

A species is a very specific taxonomic rank. In most cases, a species includes just one type of organism, and sometimes it includes a few types of organisms. Members of the same species are very closely related and share almost identical DNA. The size, weight, shape, and color of organisms in a species may be different, but most other characteristics are the same. For example, dogs belong to the species *Canis lupus*. There are many different breeds of dogs that vary in size, weight, shape, and color, but they all belong to the same species and share similar characteristics.

So what defines a species? Most scientists agree that a species is a group of organisms that can interbreed and produce <u>fertile</u> offspring. Some organisms can interbreed and produce offspring, but their offspring are <u>infertile</u>, meaning the offspring cannot reproduce. For example, when a horse and donkey interbreed, they produce an offspring called a mule. Mules cannot produce offspring. Therefore, horses and donkeys are not the same species.

Strangely enough, domestic dogs share the same species classification as the gray wolf. A gray wolf and a domestic dog could interbreed and produce fertile offspring. Scientists believe dogs descended from gray wolves but developed distinct traits, perhaps due to their domestication by humans. Because the dog has many characteristics that the gray wolf does not, scientists classify dogs as a sub-species of *Canis lupus*. This special category maintains the dog's connection to its species while acknowledging its differences. The domestic dog's sub-species name is *Canis lupus familiaris*.

1. A. What does it mean for an organism to be <u>infertile</u>?
   B. Make inferences from the text to define <u>fertile</u>.

2. What must two organisms be able to do in order to be classified as the same species?

3. Describe the rules of capitalization used when naming a species.

4. A. What is a <u>sub-species</u>?
   B. What can you infer about the meaning of the prefix "sub"?
   C. Explain why domestic dogs are a sub-species of the gray wolf.

READING INFORMATIONAL TEXT
Classifying Plants

Read the text and answer the questions.

The plant kingdom is a very diverse group of organisms. To classify plants into smaller divisions, classes, orders, families, genus, and species, scientists consider many of a plant's physical characteristics.

Some of the physical characteristics scientists use to classify plants include the type of roots it has, the shape and number of its leaves, and the height or thickness of its stem. Scientists also study how plants reproduce—does the plant produce seeds, pods, or spores? They use that information to help with classification.

Scientists also classify plants based on how they transport water. Vascular plants have a complex system of cells that transport water throughout the plant. Vascular plants like trees and shrubs can grow very tall because water can be easily transported to even the highest parts. Non-vascular plants have specialized cells that carry water to different parts of the plant. Non-vascular plants like mosses have no stems, roots, or leaves, and are usually short because they cannot transport water to a great height.

Trees, which are vascular, can be as either deciduous or coniferous. Deciduous trees, like oaks, maples, and willows, have flat leaves. Deciduous trees drop their leaves in the winter and grow new leaves in the spring. Many deciduous trees are flowering trees and many produce fruits and nuts. Coniferous trees, on the other hand, are trees that have cones and needle-like leaves. Coniferous trees, which are often called evergreens, do not drop their needles and they stay green throughout the winter.

1. A. What is the main idea of the text?
   B. What methods are used to develop and support the main idea?

2. List at least 5 ways that scientists classify plants.

3. Use a small Venn diagram to compare and contrast the following:
   A. Vascular plants and non-vascular plants
   B. Deciduous trees and coniferous trees.

4. The plant taxonomic level of "division" is most similar to which animal taxonomic level—phylum, class, order, family, genus, or species?

Classify by Leaves

Complete Parts A, B, C, and D.

PART A: In a small group, look at the different types of leaves shown. List 5-10 traits you could use to compare and contrast the leaves.

'l photos courtesy of Wikimedia Commons

PART B: In your group, decide what traits you will use to classify the leaves. Sort the leaves into 2-4 taxa, and give each taxon a name that describes its characteristics.

PART C: Compare and contrast your classification with other groups in your class. How many different ways were the leaves grouped together?

PART D: How does your classification system compare with the system that scientists use? Use an online resource if necessary.

Binomial Nomenclature

Read the text and answer the questions.

Before the 1700s, scientists had not yet agreed on one way to name living organisms. Most animals had common names like cat or dog, but using common names was confusing and made communication about organisms difficult.

One problem with common names is that they are not reliable—they can be misleading. For example, a "sea cucumber" sounds like a vegetable but it is actually an animal. A "sea horse" is not a horse at all—it is actually a fish. Another problem with common names is that some living organisms have many different common names. For example, a cougar is commonly called a puma, a catamount, and even a mountain lion. Scientists needed a reliable system of naming organisms—a <u>taxonomy</u>—that would make it easier to communicate with each other about organisms.

An early system of taxonomy used Latin words to describe what an organism looked like. However, this had problems, too. Latin names were too long and hard to remember. Also, scientists around the world often named the same organism using different Latin descriptions. Some scientists named the common briar rose *Rosa sylvestris inodora seu canina,* which means "odorless woodland dog rose" in Latin. Other scientists called the briar rose *Rosa sylvestris alba cum rubore, folio glabro* which means "pinkish-white woodland rose with hairless leaves." Scientists needed a way to make naming organisms more consistent around the world.

The system of taxonomy used today was first introduced by Carl Linnaeus, a Swedish naturalist who lived in the 1700s. He proposed that each organism be given a two-part scientific name based upon its classification. This system of naming became known as <u>binomial nomenclature</u>. The first part of any organism's name is its genus. An organism's genus name allows scientists to immediately recognize what other organisms it is related to. The second part is the organism's individual name, which allows scientists to recognize the specific individual organism. For example, a cougar's scientific classification is *Puma concolour.*

1. A. What is the primary purpose of this text?
    B. Describe the organizational structure of the text.
    C. List three benefits to the organizational structure used.

2. A. Use the text to define <u>taxonomy</u>.
    B. Describe the purpose of taxonomy.
    C. List two ways scientists benefit from the taxonomy used today.

3. Complete the graphic organizer by summarizing the problems, solution, and results presented in the text.

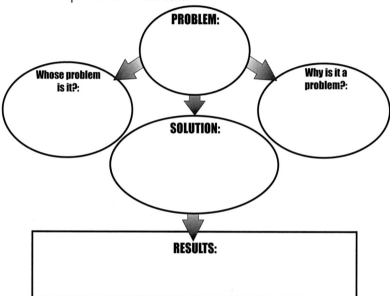

. Summarize the five 5 W's of the last paragraph.
    A. What is binomial nomenclature?
    B. Who invented it? Where, and when?
    C. Why did he invent it?

. Describe each part of the scientific names assigned to all organisms:
    A. What is each part called?
    B. What is the purpose of each part?

. The scientific name for humans is *Homo sapiens*.
    A. Which part of the name indicates the genus?
    B. Which part indicates the specific species?

. Use the text and logical reasoning to explain why each of these features might be an important quality of a good system of taxonomy:
    A. consistency   B. reliability   C. flexibility

COMPARE & CONTRAST

Bacteria and Viruses

Read the text and answer the questions.

Ask the Doctor FAQ (Frequently Asked Questions)

Q: Are viruses a type of bacteria?

A: No! Bacteria and viruses are two very different things. Bacteria are living organisms made of only a single-cell. Viruses are not made of cells and are not alive at all! A virus is simply made of proteins that contain DNA.

Q: Do bacteria and viruses do the same thing?

A: Both bacteria and viruses can affect your body but in different ways. Some bacteria live on your skin and inside your body all the time, but most bacteria in your body are essential to important processes like digestion and making vitamins. Some bacteria can be harmful and cause diseases like tuberculosis, strep throat, and salmonella. On the other hand, viruses are always harmful. Interestingly though, the cowpox virus was used in vaccinations to help prevent people from catching smallpox. Today, scientists are trying to learn how to use viruses to fight infections.

Q: Do bacteria and viruses spread the same way?

A: No. Bacteria can multiply by making copies of themselves wherever conditions are right...and most bacteria are not too picky about conditions. A virus cannot reproduce by itself, so it attaches itself to a living cell and tricks the living cell into producing more virus bodies. Unlike bacteria, a virus cannot survive by itself. It must be inside or on a living organism.

Q: Is the treatment the same when we get sick?

A: Maybe. Rest, fluids, and avoiding getting anyone else sick are good strategies whichever is the cause of your illness. Sometimes your body can fight off bacteria or a virus on its own. Sometimes you need medicine. Antibacterial medicines help your body kill the bad bacteria. Viral medicines help your body develop antibodies that interfere with how the virus works.

1. Use a Venn diagram to compare and contrast bacteria and viruses.

2. Describe the effects of bacteria and viruses on the human body

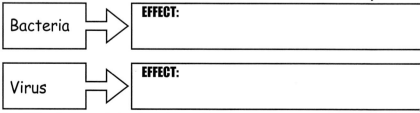

Bacteria ⟹ **EFFECT:**

Virus ⟹ **EFFECT:**

3. Why does medicine for a bacterial infection not treat a viral infection?

©Carole Marsh/Gallopade • www.gallopade.com • page 22

Binomial Names

Read the text and complete Parts A and B.

All species of living organisms are given a two-part scientific name in Latin to describe it. The Latin names of a plant or animal can sometimes tell you where the organism is typically found.

PART A: Make inferences from each organism's Latin name to guess where it is from. Choose from the list.

Japan • California • Australia
India • Brazil • Mexico • China • Italy

Scientific Name	Type of Plant	Place of Origin
Anemopsis californica	flowering desert plant	
Arum italicum	flowering plant	
Azadirachta indica	hardwood tree	
Callistephus chinensis	flowering plant	
Eriobotrya japonica	plum tree	
Geohintonia mexicana	flowering cactus	
Raddia brasiliensis	grass	
Raoulia australis	gray colored moss	

PART B: Analyze each scientific name and match it to the common name that it describes. Use your word-detective skills and look for similarities.

. _____ Pinus cembra   A. Carrot

. _____ Panthera tigris   B. Domestic cat

. _____ Papaver orientale   C. Oriental poppy

. _____ Citrus sinensis   D. Cembrian pine

. _____ Felis catus   E. Tiger

. _____ Daucus carota   F. Empress tree

. _____ Paulownia imperialis   G. Orange

Correlations to Common Core State Standards

For your convenience, correlations are listed page-by-page, and for the entire book!

This book is correlated to the Common Core State Standards for English Language Arts grades 3-8, and to Common Core State Standards for Literacy in History, Science, & Technological Subjects grades 6-8.

Correlations are highlighted in gray.

	READING	WRITING	LANGUAGE	SPEAKING & LISTENING
	Includes: RI: Reading Informational Text RST: Reading Science & Technical Subjects	*Includes:* W: Writing WHST: Writing History/Social Studies, Science, & Technical Subjects	*Includes:* L: Language LF: Language Foundational Skills	*Includes:* SL: Speaking & Listening

PAGE #	RI / RST	W / WHST	L / LF	SL
2	1 2 3 4 5 6 7 8 9 10	1 2 3 4 5 6 7 8 9 10	1 2 3 4 5 6	1 2 3 4 5 6
3	1 2 3 4 5 6 7 8 9 10	1 2 3 4 5 6 7 8 9 10	1 2 3 4 5 6	1 2 3 4 5 6
4	1 2 3 4 5 6 7 8 9 10	1 2 3 4 5 6 7 8 9 10	1 2 3 4 5 6	1 2 3 4 5 6
5	1 2 3 4 5 6 7 8 9 10	1 2 3 4 5 6 7 8 9 10	1 2 3 4 5 6	1 2 3 4 5 6
6-7	1 2 3 4 5 6 7 8 9 10	1 2 3 4 5 6 7 8 9 10	1 2 3 4 5 6	1 2 3 4 5 6
8-9	1 2 3 4 5 6 7 8 9 10	1 2 3 4 5 6 7 8 9 10	1 2 3 4 5 6	1 2 3 4 5 6
10-11	1 2 3 4 5 6 7 8 9 10	1 2 3 4 5 6 7 8 9 10	1 2 3 4 5 6	1 2 3 4 5 6
12-13	1 2 3 4 5 6 7 8 9 10	1 2 3 4 5 6 7 8 9 10	1 2 3 4 5 6	1 2 3 4 5 6
14-15	1 2 3 4 5 6 7 8 9 10	1 2 3 4 5 6 7 8 9 10	1 2 3 4 5 6	1 2 3 4 5 6
16	1 2 3 4 5 6 7 8 9 10	1 2 3 4 5 6 7 8 9 10	1 2 3 4 5 6	1 2 3 4 5 6
17	1 2 3 4 5 6 7 8 9 10	1 2 3 4 5 6 7 8 9 10	1 2 3 4 5 6	1 2 3 4 5 6
18	1 2 3 4 5 6 7 8 9 10	1 2 3 4 5 6 7 8 9 10	1 2 3 4 5 6	1 2 3 4 5 6
19	1 2 3 4 5 6 7 8 9 10	1 2 3 4 5 6 7 8 9 10	1 2 3 4 5 6	1 2 3 4 5 6
20-21	1 2 3 4 5 6 7 8 9 10	1 2 3 4 5 6 7 8 9 10	1 2 3 4 5 6	1 2 3 4 5 6
22	1 2 3 4 5 6 7 8 9 10	1 2 3 4 5 6 7 8 9 10	1 2 3 4 5 6	1 2 3 4 5 6
23	1 2 3 4 5 6 7 8 9 10	1 2 3 4 5 6 7 8 9 10	1 2 3 4 5 6	1 2 3 4 5 6
COMPLETE BOOK	1 2 3 4 5 6 7 8 9 10	1 2 3 4 5 6 7 8 9 10	1 2 3 4 5 6	1 2 3 4 5 6

For the complete Common Core standard identifier, combine your grade + "." + letter code above + "." + number code above.

In addition to the correlations indicated here, the activities may be adapted or expanded to align to additional standards and to meet the diverse needs of your unique students!